My Step-Dad's Brother

Fiona Davenport

Copyright

Chapter 1

Harrison

The rapid clicks of the camera were a comforting sound to me. It was familiar, a constant in my life when everything else was ever changing.

As a photo-journalist for a respected magazine, I spent most of my time traveling to new places. It was my job to document the events of the world through pictures. Sometimes, my assignments were full of adrenaline and danger. Other times, I immersed myself in the local cultures, an extended vacation that earned me a paycheck. I had even spent days alone with wild animals, not speaking to another soul until I left their company.

No matter the job, though, it kept me on the move and I loved every minute of it. And, everywhere I went, the purr of the shutter on my camera went with me.

Lowering the lens, I looked up at the sky and then back at the scene I was photographing. The sun was fading, and I was about to lose my light. Quickly clicking through my digital screen, I nodded to myself, satisfied that the perfect shot was among them. Carefully, I packed away my equipment, my eyes often straying to the party below the bluff where I was perched.

This small town on an uncharted island in the South Pacific had a rich culture, and I was grateful at their open and friendly manner, allowing me to immortalize them through my camera.

A young couple danced in the center of a large circle of people. Their clothes were bright and decadent, befitting a bride and groom. They gazed into each other's eyes with such love, I felt a slight pang in my chest. My lifestyle wasn't exactly conducive to relationships, and I'd never been interested in one-night stands. I was married to the job. And at thirty, I still had a lot of years left to devote to it. But lately, I'd begun to feel an odd restlessness, a longing that I didn't quite recognize or even understand.

Heading down to the village, I dropped my equipment in my hut and joined the celebration. It reminded me that it wouldn't be long before I'd be attending my older brother's nuptials in the states.

I drove through the small town of Fentonville, Florida, and looked all around. My face twisted in disgust, the photographer in me noting the lack of anything remotely interesting to take a picture of. It was sleepy and boring. Perfect for my brother, Stanley.

As I pulled up to the address he'd given me, I had to laugh. Stanley had warned me that his fiancée, whom everyone called Bunny apparently, was a bit of a free spirit. Which was quite a shock coming from a man who'd spent his entire life coloring inside the lines with ultimate precision.

Now, I was even more blown away by his choice. Not disappointed, though, my stodgy brother needed some spark in his life. The small house was painted pink, not overly ostentatious, but bright enough to stand out among the drab surroundings. The yard had large, plastic flowers on metal sticks stuck haphazardly around it and . . . I blinked. Yep, there was also a flamingo.

There was also a small flower bed that was perfectly manicured, clean and organized with complimenting colors. It seemed a little out of place until I remembered Stanley mentioning that his soon-to-be step-daughter was much different than her mother.

I would have plenty of time to get to know my new niece in the coming weeks. Stanley had asked me to extend my trip here for the wedding and stay while they went on a honeymoon. Bunny's daughter was still in high school and they didn't want to leave her completely alone for two whole weeks. She didn't graduate for a few months yet and like most parents, it was clear they wouldn't see their child as an adult until graduation. I didn't mind, though, it felt good to take a break, even if it meant being caged in this tiny town with my young, soon-to-be niece.

Magnolia Bloom. A real flower-power name, I chuckled to myself. She probably hated it. A picture of a gangly teen with wild, curly hair, ripped up jeans, and glasses that were too big for her face, conjured in my mind. It just seemed to fit the name.

I parked my cherry red, Charger convertible in the driveway, next to a sliver Prius hybrid. It was one thing I kept, along with my small studio apartment in Miami, though, I never spent much time with either. Turning off the car, I grabbed a bag from the back seat and hopped out. I shut the door and rounded the front of both cars to reach a walkway that led to a white front door. I pressed the door bell and almost laughed out loud when I heard the chime through the door playing *Walking on Sunshine*.

When it opened, I was greeted by a plump, pixie-like woman smiling brightly at me.

"Harrison?" she asked in a high, musical voice vibrating with excitement.

I grinned and tipped an invisible hat. "The one and only."

"I'm Bunny. Welcome! Welcome!" She practically threw herself into my arms and hugged me tightly. "We are so glad you're here!" When she released me, she turned and called into the house, "Stanley! Magnolia! Harrison is here!" Then she slipped her arm through mine and led me into the house.

I saw my brother first, his tall, sturdy stature, slightly graying, dark brown hair, and serious brown eyes. Except, I saw more life in them than I had ever seen before and it filled me with joy. Stanley was fifteen years older than me and after our dad took off when I was four, he practically raised me. He was strong, steadfast, and responsible, providing me and our mother with a stable home.

We'd had our disagreements about my "nomadic existence" and "unpredictable job," but I'd seen the scrapbook he kept of my articles and published photos. He supported me, despite his constant worry. No one deserved to find love and happiness more than he did.

"Harrison." His smile was wide as he approached and shook my hand heartily. I was tempted to pull him into a hug, just to ruffle his proper feathers. He hadn't ever been one for physical displays of affection, though, he showed how much he cared in many other ways.

However, my jaw practically slammed into the light wood floor when he stepped back and pulled Bunny into his embrace, tucking her into his side. I almost fell over when he kissed her temple and smiled at her like a lovesick boy. As my surprise wore off, the little devil inside me grinned evilly. Oh, man, this was going to be so much fun. All out of brotherly love, of course.

"I see you met my beautiful Bunny," he said as he tore his eyes from her to look at me again. My eyes were still wide and, holy shit, my brother was fucking blushing. I had to bite back a litany of teasing comments, there would be plenty of time for that later.

"Seems to me like that name fits you better," I drawled. "When did you become so soft and cuddly?" Okay, so I let one slide.

He straightened his spine and cleared his throat. "I don't know what you mean, Harrison." Soft and cuddly didn't seem to have come with a sense of humor.

A noise behind the couple drew my attention and I looked up to see a girl walking down a set of stairs on my left. When she hit the bottom step, I froze. My heart stopped beating, the world stopped spinning, and time ceased to exist.

Mine.

The word reverberated in my head, bouncing around and growing until it filled every nook and crevice. When everything started moving again, it did so at an elevated pace. My heart rate soared, and I felt a little dizzy.

This close, I realized I'd been mistaken. She wasn't a girl. She was all woman. I tried hard to keep my gaze on her shoulder length, silvery blonde hair, huge, clear blue eyes, and rosy lips. I failed spectacularly. She was wearing a wide-necked, purple T-shirt and my eyes were drawn down the long column of her throat to large, full breasts that I immediately knew would spill from my hands. My eyes continued to her white shorts that showcased her nipped in waist and luscious, rounded hips, all the way down her endless legs to the most adorable, purple painted toes I'd ever seen.

We'd be having a talk about those shorts, I thought darkly. While I enjoyed the assets they so clearly highlighted, I didn't want any other men looking at what was mine.

She was several inches taller than her mother and her face was longer, but otherwise, they looked very much alike. Movement in my peripheral vision snapped me out of my inappropriate perusal of my teenage niece's body. My eyes whipped up and I only hoped that neither Stanley or Bunny had noticed me ogling Magnolia. I turned back to them, trying to avoid the matching mixture of lust and shock in her eyes.

Mine.

No.

Seventeen, Harrison. Still in high school. Can't be traveling the world if you're locked in a jail cell, man.

Luckily, the couple was gazing at Magnolia fondly and it didn't seem like they had noticed my reaction. I shifted my bag strategically in front of me, hiding the physical evidence of said reaction.

"This is my daughter, Magnolia," Bunny introduced.

"Maggie," she corrected softly. Her voice was husky and it washed over me, hardening my cock even more. "It's nice to meet you, Harrison. Stanley has told us a lot about you."

I forced an easy smile. "I'm sure none of it is true," I joked. She smiled and my breath caught.

Mine.

Fuck. My shoulders slumped, I had to stop that.

"Come into the kitchen," Bunny suggested as she waved to a door behind her. "We were about to sit down to a special dinner. I'm so glad you could be here to join us! We're celebrating Magnolia's"—"Maggie" her daughter interrupted to scold her—"birthday today, even though it's not until tomorrow. With the rehearsal dinner and everything, Stanley very smartly suggested making tonight about our girl. You only turn eighteen once!" She fluttered over to Maggie and kissed her cheek, then flitted through the door she'd indicated.

"Happy Birthday," I murmured, keeping my eyes averted as I followed Bunny. It was no use, I couldn't keep from admiring Maggie's spectacular ass. *Tomorrow.* She would be eighteen tomorrow. Midnight. Eighteen. My body started to burn as images of our naked bodies passionately entwined filled my mind. Those legs wrapped around me as I pumped my hips, burying myself inside her over and over. Making her mine.

I shook my head, trying to dispel the fantasies, but they wouldn't go away completely. Neither would one other thought.

At midnight, she's mine.

Chapter 2
Maggie

Oh.

My.

Hotness.

When I'd started down the stairs at my mom's yell, I'd been excited to meet my soon-to-be step-dad's brother. It had been just Mom and me for so long, but not anymore. Her marriage to Stanley meant we had a family. Having family meant my mom had other people she could depend on when I left home, although, I wasn't sure how much help my new uncle was going to be since he spent so much time traveling the world. The lucky jerk. I'd never even managed to make it to Miami and it was only a couple of hours away from the small town where I'd been raised.

My best friend, Lilah, and I had always talked about taking off to see the world after graduation. But, she had moved to New York when we were fourteen so her mom could undergo cancer treatments. We still dreamed about it from time to time, but I think we'd also accepted that it would never be more than that. I was envious of this guy who'd seen the world.

All thoughts of Lilah, my mom, Stanley, and travel were wiped from my brain the moment I laid eyes on Harrison Butler. My heart started pounding in my chest. My stomach felt like a swarm of butterflies had taken flight inside it. And my panties? I wouldn't have been surprised to learn that they'd spontaneously combusted at the sight of him. But in my defense, I hadn't been prepared for the reality of him, not when I'd been thinking of him as my uncle.

At six foot two, with a lean frame and sinewy muscles, he seemed to vibrate with an inner energy. His hair was as dark as the sky at midnight, and long enough that there was a hint of curl to it. His whiskey-brown eyes were surrounded by thick lashes that any woman would kill to have. His skin was golden brown, probably from spending lots of time outside. The only lines in his face were from laughter, and judging by the looks of them, he laughed a lot.

He was male, all male, and nothing like the boys at school. For the first time in my life, I responded like a woman. I'd never desired any of the boys at my school, but

I'd read and heard enough to know that was exactly what I was feeling for Harrison. I wanted him. Badly.

If the heated look in his light brown eyes for the brief moment they'd met mine was any indication, he wanted me right back. As I followed everyone into the kitchen, my cheeks heated as I remembered how he'd yanked his bag in front of his body after his gaze had scanned mine—like he'd been trying to hide something. Only he wasn't going to be able to hide it from me forever because I fully intended to use the next couple of weeks to their full advantage.

I chuckled under my breath as I sat down, thinking about how much I'd argued against the idea of having my new uncle stay with me while Mom and Stanley went on their honeymoon. I'd been so pissed off that they thought I needed a babysitter after all the years I'd taken care of my mom, but Stanley refused to hear any of it. Not even when my mom tried explaining to him that I'd be eighteen by then and fine on my own.

"What's so funny, Magnolia?" my mom asked as she set the lasagna on the table.

"Oh, I was just thinking how funny it is, the way things turn out sometimes." As in, it was a lucky thing Stanley was a bit of a stick in the mud, or else I wouldn't have Harrison all to myself soon. Which was quite ironic when you thought about it because the odds were high that he'd throw a fit when he found out about Harrison and me.

Harrison and me. Yeah, I might have been jumping the gun a bit picturing us as a couple already, but I couldn't find it in myself to care. It didn't matter to me that he was thirty to my soon-to-be eighteen. Or that I wasn't even out of high school yet for another few months, and he was a renowned photo-journalist for a fancy magazine. Or even that he was the brother of the man my mom was going to marry this weekend. The only thing I cared about was the bone-deep knowledge that this man was meant to be mine.

She dropped a kiss on the top of my head as she placed a basket of garlic bread on the table before sitting down with us. "How so, my flower girl?"

I looked across the table, my eyes locking with Harrison's while my mom dished food out onto everyone's plates. "Just think about it. Harrison's a world traveler, but he's going to stay here with me in this sleepy town while you and Stanley head off on your honeymoon adventure. It's like they're trading places."

"There's nothing wrong with this sleepy town," Stanley grumbled.

"Of course not, honey bear," my mom cooed across the table at him. "But that doesn't mean we can't be excited about our trip to Italy, now does it?"

"How can I not be when you're so delighted by it?"

"Only because you're taking me on my dream trip."

The way he looked at my mom had my eyes filling with tears. When I'd first met Stanley, I'd been worried that he was all wrong for her. He was ultra conservative and my mom was such a free spirit. But there wasn't a doubt in my mind about them as a couple anymore because he showed her—and me—how very much he loved her.

I was sniffling a little when I felt something brush softly against my leg. A quick glance under the table had my head jerking up to stare across it at Harrison because it had been his foot I'd found there. His eyes were filled with concern… and was that anger I saw, too?

"Why're you crying, Maggie?" His voice was a low rasp that sent goosebumps along my skin.

"Happy tears," I hiccupped, waving him off, even as my heart raced at the look he was sending my way.

"My girl." Mom sighed, reaching over and squeezing my hand. "She's got such a good head on her shoulders. Straight A's all through school. Never caused a single bit of trouble. But she's also got the softest heart of anyone I know."

"Which she got from her mother," Stanley interjected. "Both my girls are sensitive souls."

I snorted softly, knowing darn well that even though I had a soft heart, I wasn't a 'sensitive soul' as he'd put it. Maybe I would have been, if I hadn't have spent the last ten years taking care of business around the house. Making sure the bills were paid since my mom could be flighty like that. Someone had to live in the real world, and as much as I loved my mom, I knew it wasn't going to be her.

"I don't like seeing those pretty blue eyes filled with tears." Harrison's foot slid along the side of my leg again, offering comfort.

"Oh, you'll get used to it," my mom replied airily.

"Not if I have anything to say about it." I saw, more than heard, his words since he spoke so lowly. But with my eyes on his lush lips, I knew what he'd said and my heart soared.

"Hush, Bunny." The smile Stanley sent my mom's way was soft. "Or else you'll scare my brother off before we make it to the airport, and then what'll we do? We can't just leave Maggie here alone for two weeks."

It was at this point in the conversation that I usually interjected with all the reasons they could do exactly that, but this time around I didn't say anything. Now that I'd met him, I didn't want to risk Stanley having a sudden about-face and deciding Harrison didn't need to stay with me.

Stanley offered his brother an apologetic smile. "It means a lot to me that you agreed to stay here with Maggie, especially since I know how much you hate small towns like Fentonville."

"Which just means they already have something in common," my mom mumbled after she polished off her last bite of garlic bread.

"You're not a fan of small towns, either?" Harrison asked me.

"Well, I've never really been anywhere other than a small town, but I've always dreamed of traveling," I answered shyly, feeling like a stupid teenager as I admitted it.

But Harrison didn't seem to mind at all. "Maybe I'll take you to Miami next weekend, show you the sights."

"Now, Harrison. She's only seventeen."

"Eighteen," I interjected.

Stanley smiled at me a little ruefully. "Yes, sorry. It's hard to think of my step-daughter being eighteen." He turned back to Harrison. "Anyway, anything could happen to her in a city like Miami," Stanley chided.

"Nothing bad will happen to her when she's with me. Ever." I shivered at the dark tone in his voice, as though he was ready to fight some imaginary foe to protect me.

"Of course not. I'm sure Harrison will take wonderful care of Magnolia for us," my mom agreed, jumping up from the table to get the cake off the counter.

As she set it in front of me, my eyes met Harrison's one last time before I looked down at the lit candles. Then I closed them and made my wish.

Please let Harrison want me as much as I want him.

Chapter 3
Harrison

It was great to see Bunny and Maggie pulling out another side of Stanley. Just moving in with her had been unexpected of my very traditional brother.

I was grateful for that change because otherwise, I'd most likely have been staying at his place until after the wedding. In one short evening, I was so addicted to Maggie that the thought of being away from her for any length of time had my blood boiling. I wanted to steal her away and have her all to myself. But, I only had to wait two days until we'd be alone. Two fucking days.

Every move Maggie made, every word she spoke, had my dick vehemently disagreeing with the wait. After dinner, we went into the living room to watch a movie. Bunny and Stanley sat on the couch, his arm around her and pulling her close. I sat on the love seat along the next wall. My eyes tracked Maggie's every step when she entered the room.

She glanced at a purple, over-stuffed recliner, then at the empty spot next to me. One of her hands played with the ends of her hair, curling it round her finger as she contemplated her options. I held my breath, both hoping and dreading that she would sit next to me. It would be sweet torture to have her so near and not be able to touch her.

Finally, she ran her hands through her hair and approached me, taking the seat next to me on the small sofa. There were only a few inches between us and I set my hand down, right in the middle. I could feel the heat radiating from her body through the thin, white material of her shorts. I wanted to slip my fingers inside and see if her pussy was slick. I'd have bet my next paycheck that she was fucking soaked.

I shifted and brought one leg up to rest my ankle on the opposite knee. It gave me a little more room in the groin area and hid my reaction to Maggie from her parents. However, her beautiful blue eyes drifted over, and a sweet pink blush stained her cheeks. She smirked her porn star lips and raised an eyebrow at me. Fuck.

I quickly turned to the movie and tried to think about anything but the sexy as fuck woman sitting next to me. And those lips. Wrapped around my—shit.

Seventeen. Seventeen. Seventeen. I kept repeating to myself. It wasn't working. My cock knew she would be eighteen in a few hours. I managed to half pay attention to the movie, though, I couldn't tell you what it was about.

When the credits rolled, I breathed a sigh of relief. Except, when Stanley and Bunny stood up, Maggie didn't move.

"I'm not tired, I'm going to stay up a little longer," she said to her mother.

Bunny nodded and came over to kiss her cheek. "Not too late. We have a big day tomorrow." Then she turned to me and smiled brightly. "You're in the guest bedroom on this floor, Harrison. There is a bathroom and it's all stocked, but let me or Maggie know if you need anything."

I forced a relaxed smile. Maggie was what I needed, but what I said was, "I'll definitely do that."

Bunny and Stanley said goodnight and went upstairs for the night. I slowly turned to face Maggie. She was playing with the ends of her hair again as she watched me with a mixture of hunger and apprehension. Her innocence was clear, and a huge fucking turn on. But, she also had a confidence about her that was just as appealing.

"You want to travel someday?" I asked, breaking the ice. Not without an ulterior motive.

Maggie's face lit up and her mouth widened into a grin. She was so damn gorgeous. "Oh yes. I've always wanted to take off and see the world." Her cheeks turned pink again and she dropped her head down, but looked up at me through her long lashes. "I wish you could take me with you on some of your adventures," she mumbled shyly.

This girl was perfect. "You don't want to go to college?" I wanted to take Maggie with me when I left, but I found myself determined to make sure she followed her dreams. I'd have to take a leave of absence from my job so I could stay at home with her while she finished high school. If she wanted to continue her education, I could put in for local assignments until she graduated.

"No," she said softly. "I've only ever wanted to travel and..." she trailed off. She brought her knees up, hugging them to her chest and began playing with her hair again.

I reached out to capture her hand. "And what? You can tell me anything, Maggie."

Her eyes went soft and she smiled sweetly. "Well, it may seem odd since I've spent most of my life caring for my mom, but I've—um, I really just want to be a mom." She studied me anxiously after finishing. Did she think I would laugh?

I ran a finger down her nose and across her velvety lips. "I think that's great, baby doll. You'll be an amazing mother." She flushed with delight and hugged her legs tighter. I tugged her arms apart and then put both of my hands on the tops of her knees. "I can make all of that happen for you," I purred. I hadn't meant to let that slip out, but I was having a hard time concentrating. The way she was sitting, if I just . . . I pressed her legs apart, baring her center to my gaze. She gasped, and I glanced up to see her blue pools swirling with curiosity and desire.

"Are you a virgin, Maggie?" I asked quietly. It wouldn't make me want her any less if she wasn't, but I couldn't help hoping that I would be the only one to ever see, taste, and be inside her. She nodded and I swallowed hard, resisting the urge to shout to anyone listening that this girl was mine. All fucking mine.

Running a finger along the seam of her shorts, I exhaled heavily and rasped, "I knew you'd be wet for me, baby doll." The white material between her legs was drenched. I could smell her arousal and it was fucking intoxicating. "Looks like these shorts are ruined. Good thing you weren't ever going to wear them again." Finding the right spot, I put pressure on the little nub I knew was hidden in beneath the fabric. She gasped again and instinctively tried to close her legs. I growled and kept them open, circling the area again with one digit.

She whimpered, and I knew I was one sound away from ripping her clothes off and latching my mouth onto her pussy. Quickly, I closed her legs and turned them so they dropped to the floor. She started to say something, but I held up my hand for silence. I needed a minute.

Closing my eyes, I took deep breaths and counted, focusing hard on each number until I finally had myself under control. I was still hard as fucking steel, but at least I knew I wouldn't lose it and take her on the fucking floor.

I stood and pulled her up with me. "Good night, Maggie." I kissed her forehead before turning her to face the room's entrance and patting her plump ass to get her moving.

She put up a little resistance and turned her head to look at me with surprise. "But— I don't understand. Don't you want—"

"Fuck, yes, I want," I growled. I kissed her forehead again to soften my response and chuckled. "That doesn't mean I'm going to give in and make one of us a felon in most states. Now go on to bed and we'll talk more about all of this after the wedding."

She was staring up at me with those big, clear blue eyes, so full of want and I couldn't resist. I pulled her into my arms and crushed my mouth over hers. Her arms locked around my neck and she molded her body to mine. It felt fucking fantastic and I was desperate to taste her. I skimmed my tongue across the seam of her lips and she immediately opened for me. I groaned and held her tighter with my hands splayed on her back, as my tongue pushed in and tangled with hers.

After a minute, I tore myself away and stepped back, keeping her at arm's length. "Upstairs, baby doll."

She licked her lips and I almost gave in to kissing her again but before I did, she spun around and jogged up the stairs.

My gaze drifted to the digital clock on the night stand for the millionth time since I'd gone to bed. *One AM.* Then I returned to staring at the ceiling. *One AM.*

She'd been eighteen for an hour. It took everything I had in me to keep from sneaking up the stairs to claim Maggie. I turned on my side, away from the clock, and punched my pillow, trying to get comfortable. My wood was making it very difficult.

A sound reached my ears and I sat up in bed, looking in the direction from which it came. It was the creak of my door opening. Moonlight was streaming in through a set of glass doors that went out to a patio and it cast a glow over Maggie as she slipped inside the room.

She looked fucking amazing. She was wearing a long, thin, sleep shirt that stretched across her breasts. Her beaded nipples were poking through, making my mouth water.

"What are you doing here, baby doll?" My voice was gruff and too late, I realized how harsh it sounded. Her body froze, the smile on her face slipping and her shoulders sagging.

"Sorry," she whispered, and started to turn.

"Maggie." I intended to soothe her worry, assure her I still wanted her and send her back to bed.

She looked back at me over her shoulder and the sight was so innocently seductive, I found myself holding out my hand instead, as my good intentions flew out the window. Her gaze dropped to it and then a sweet smile once again graced her face as she padded over to me.

I sat up and swung my feet over the side of the bed. Taking her wrists, I tugged her forward until she was forced to climb onto my lap, straddling me. Her T-shirt rode up her thick thighs and I saw a peek of underwear between her legs. Thank fuck. I was also extremely grateful that I'd chosen to sleep in my boxer briefs, instead of naked. Both layers of underwear weren't much protection, but it was something.

Sliding my hands up her legs and under her top, I held her at the waist. Her heated skin burned the pads of my fingers and sent sparks of electricity throughout my entire body.

"I'm sorry, babe." I punctuated my apology with a kiss to the tip of her nose. "I didn't mean to sound angry. It's just that I want you so much, having you here is torture."

"But, it's after midnight," she said, scooting close until her tits were pressed against me, those hard little peaks digging into my chest. "I'm eighteen."

I couldn't resist a kiss on her plush lips, getting a small taste to hold me over until I could feast. She moaned and squirmed, prompting me to tighten my grip on her and keep her from moving around on my cock. I was hard enough as it was.

"Patience, Maggie," I chuckled. "Now isn't the right time. I don't want to have to rush. When we are finally going to be together, I'm going to explore every inch of this sinful body. I'll make sure that your first time is incredible."

She moaned and her lips searched out mine. We made out like teenagers for the next ten minutes. My hand glided down from her waist to dip inside her panties and swipe through her slit.

I groaned at the feel of her arousal, it was drenched. She shuddered as I ran my finger up and down. After a few rotations around her clit, I bought my finger to my mouth and sucked it inside. Maggie watched me with hooded eyes and moaned, "Harrison."

Hearing my name fall from her lips was more than I could take. I grabbed her ass and stood, swiftly pivoting and laying her down gently on the bed. Unlocking her legs from around my waist, I let them fall over the side. Then I dropped to my knees and pushed her legs open wide. I leaned in and took a deep inhale. "You smell delicious, baby doll, and you taste even better. I need more of your sweetness on my tongue."

Slowly, I dragged her panties down and off, tossing them onto the nightstand. Her shirt had already ridden up so I had an unobstructed view of her sex. "So pretty," I murmured. "Pink and so wet." I lowered my head and dragged my tongue up her center.

"Yesss!" she hissed. I grinned to myself. My Maggie may have been untouched, but it was obvious that there was a sexual tigress hiding out inside her. I fully intended to bring her out in full force, eventually. And, I had a feeling my girl would be loud. Just the thought of her shouting my name as she came had pre-come leaking from my tip. But, for now, I'd have to keep her quiet.

"Hush, baby doll. We don't want your parents to hear me eating your sweet little pussy. Can you be quiet?"

I looked up to see Maggie biting her lip and when our eyes met, her head jerked up and down. I smiled and kissed her pelvis. "Good girl." Then I went back to work on her, licking and sucking until she was shaking with need. She whimpered and I stopped, giving her a warning look.

Her lips formed a thin, straight line and she clenched her jaw. Returning to my task, I added a finger to my ministrations. "Fuck, Maggie, you're so tight. I'm going to need to stretch you so you can take all of me." I worked her until I was able to fit a second finger inside. Fuck, she was snug, and come dripped from my dick as I imagined what it would feel like to replace those digits with my cock.

Pumping my fingers in and out, licking, suckling, and a bite here and there, had her primed and about to fall. She whimpered, so I reached up and clapped a hand over her mouth before curling my fingers and drawing her little clit into my mouth. Her muffled scream shot fire straight to my groin and I almost came right along with her.

I worked her through her shudders until the feel of her pulse on my tongue had evened out. Then I kissed each thigh before getting to my feet. Pulling her shirt down, I helped her move so she was lying fully on the bed and I could climb in next to her. I gathered her in my arms and held her close, tucking her face into my neck and kissing the top of her head. "Next time," I grunted. "I'm going to have your cherry, baby doll." Her hand drifted down to palm my erection and I quickly caught the limb and brought it up to brush my lips across the back. "Next time."

It didn't take long for her breath to even out, but I stayed awake, holding her, and wishing I didn't have to send her back to her own bed. At around four in the morning, I kissed her softly. "Wake up, baby doll. You need to get back to your own bed before someone finds us in here together." She groaned and burrowed deeper into my chest, making me chuckle. She was so damn cute.

It took me a good ten minutes to rouse her enough to get her up and moving. I walked with her to the door and pulled her into my arms for a lingering kiss. It would have to hold us for a while. "Good night, sweet Maggie," I whispered.

Chapter 4
Maggie

"Wakey, wakey, eggs and bakey."

I woke up to my mom's sing-song voice. Opening bleary eyes, I found her standing at my doorway. Considering I barely remembered leaving Harrison's bed down the hall a few hours ago, it was quite startling. I lifted my hand to my chest and was happy to find I was wearing my usual sleep shirt, so there wasn't anything out of the norm to make her suspicious. Or I didn't think there was, until I scooted down the bed a little and realized I wasn't wearing any panties.

"Breakfast's ready, sleepy head," she continued. "Now that you're up, I'll go wake Harrison so we can enjoy a quiet family moment before the insanity begins."

"No!" I yelped, jumping off the mattress as I remembered exactly where my panties were—smack dab on top of the nightstand in Harrison's room. My mom was oblivious most of the time, but I doubted she'd miss seeing them when she went in to wake him up. It wasn't as if she was blind, after all.

"Oh, dear. Are you okay, Magnolia?"

"Yes, sorry. Didn't mean to startle you," I breathed out, wrapping my arms around her waist after she moved forward to give me a hug. "It's just that today and tomorrow should be all about you. Why don't you head downstairs, get yourself a mug of tea, and I'll make sure Harrison is up before I join you and dish up breakfast?"

She bent down to squeeze me tightly before stepping away to look at me with tear-filled eyes. "I'm not sure what I ever did to deserve such an amazing daughter, but I'm so grateful for you either way."

Guilt stabbed me in the gut as I watched her walk away since tricking her into letting me wake Harrison up wasn't amazing. Not at all. In fact, it was the opposite, considering he was my soon-to-be uncle who'd given me my first orgasm. I wanted to keep that from my mom until I was more certain what was going to happen between Harrison and me. My motives were purely selfish, but I couldn't find it in myself to feel too guilty about it. Not with the way he made me feel last night—and in the wee hours of the morning.

I rushed through getting ready. A quick brush of my teeth and hair. Tossing on some clothes. A swipe of cherry flavored lip gloss. Then I went down to Harrison's room and knocked softly on the door before cracking it open to peek my head inside. My breath stilled in my chest when I found him sprawled on the mattress, shirtless, and with the sheet wrapped around his lean hips.

I'd felt all those sun-kissed inches of skin on his chest under my fingers, but I hadn't really had the chance to appreciate them. There hadn't been much light, only the moonlight streaming in through the glass doors. Even if it had been as bright as it was this morning, I didn't think it would have mattered because it hadn't taken long before I'd been unable to concentrate on anything other than what we'd been doing. Those long, drugging kisses. Our tongues tangled together, the taste of him filling my mouth. And then the feel of his mouth on my—um—down there, after he'd flipped me onto my back. It had been better than anything I'd ever imagined.

A quick glance at the nightstand made me gasp lightly. My panties were nowhere to be found. But then I caught a glimpse of pale pink peeking out from under the pillowcase, right next to Harrison's arm. Shutting the door behind me as softly as I could, I crept forward and whispered, "Harrison."

"Maggie," he murmured sleepily, his voice low and raspy.

Just the sound of him saying my name had me wanting to climb in beside him, but that wasn't an option with my mom and his brother waiting for us in the kitchen. Which meant I needed to do something quick so I didn't fall victim to the temptation he presented. "Whatcha doing with my panties?"

Was that a little hint of pink rising up on his cheeks as he tucked them deeper under the pillow?

"Mine," he growled, reaching his arm out and wrapping his hand around my waist to pull me towards him.

"Harrison," I breathed out. "We can't. Mom and Stanley are up. Breakfast is ready, and I convinced my mom to let me wake you up because I thought she'd find my panties on your nightstand and the jig would be up. Little did I know you slept with them after you shuffled me out of your room."

"Wanted the smell of you around me while I slept."

"Oh my goodness." There went the panties I'd just slipped on not even five minutes ago. Drenched by the words he rasped, making it even harder not to join him in the bed just so he could remove this pair the same way he had the other ones.

"Gimme a kiss, and then I'll let you go."

I leaned down and rubbed my lips against his for a brief moment before his hands fisted my hair. Then he took over, tilting my head as he plundered my mouth until I was panting for breath and shaking with need.

"Mmm, cherry." His tongue flicked out to swipe across his bottom lip after he pulled away. "Were you thinking about the one I'm gonna pop soon when you picked out your lip gloss?"

"Ummm," I gulped. I hadn't been, but I couldn't seem to form any words.

"You better head out before your mom or my brother come here looking for you and get more than they bargained for."

"Uh-huh," I agreed dazedly.

"Go on, baby doll." He turned me around and gave me a little swat on my butt. "I'll be right behind you."

The rest of the day flew by in a whirlwind of activity. I made about a million phone calls, making sure everything was in order for the rehearsal dinner tonight and the wedding tomorrow. I answered just about as many questions since everyone knew I was the point person instead of the bride. My mom wasn't quick to make decisions, so it was easier for me to handle stuff for her since I knew what she liked.

Luckily, the rehearsal went off without a hitch—unless you considered me staring at Harrison the whole time a hitch. It had been impossible for me to pull my eyes away from him as he stood next to Stanley on the opposite side of the aisle from my mom and me. With his whiskey colored orbs locked on mine, I listened with half an ear to the directions the minister was giving. It wasn't until my mom flung her arm around my shoulder to lead me forward that I even realized the rehearsal was over and it was time to head to the restaurant.

I'd requested a private dining room when I'd made the arrangements at the restaurant where Stanley had taken my mom for their first date. It was a quaint little Italian place that served the most amazing pasta in town, and since I'd gone to school with the owner's son since Kindergarten, I knew they'd make it super special for my mom. And boy, had I been right. Our group was seated at a long table covered with a crisp white cloth. There were three centerpieces filled with a wild array of colorful flowers, and each place setting had a deep purple charger plate in front of it. Mine and my mom's favorite color.

"It's perfect!" she squealed, settling into her seat in the middle of the table. Stanley was to her right, and I was to her left. As the best man, Harrison was seated next to his brother, two too many seats away from me.

The waiter came around with a bottle of champagne, filling everyone's glasses, including mine. "A toast!" Harrison called out, rising to his feet and moving to stand behind my mom and his brother, with his hand resting on the back of my chair. His fingers brushed against my neck, making me shiver as I lifted my glass in the air along with everyone else.

Stanley's eyes shot to my glass and then to my mom. He leaned over and whispered in her ear, and she reached out to snatch the champagne away from me. She took a big gulp out of it, drinking about half the contents, and then handed it back to me. "There, a tiny bit won't hurt now that you're eighteen."

Harrison leaned low and whispered in my ear, "I'll make sure one of our first stops is France so you can have all the champagne you want."

I leaned back, my eyes on him as he made his toast and moved back to his seat. Through the appetizers, the main course, and dessert, I found my neck craning in his direction often, so I could catch a glimpse of him. Each time I did, it was as though a sensor went off and he looked right back at me. After a couple of hours, dinner was finally over and I was following my mom and Stanley out of the restaurant, with Harrison right behind me, when I heard my name called out. Turning to look to the right, I caught sight of a familiar face before I was wrapped up in a hug that lasted only about a half of a second before Enzo, the owner's son and a childhood friend, was ripped away from me.

"What the hell?" he grunted.

"Get your hands off her," Harrison growled, holding Enzo by his collar.

A quick glance over my shoulder showed me that my mom and Stanley had already made it out the door. I heaved a deep sigh of relief before focusing on the situation at hand. Laying my hand on Harrison's upper arm, I stepped forward until I was right next to him. "It's okay. Enzo's a friend from school."

Harrison narrowed his eyes, flicking a glance between the two of us and I shook my head no. "Friends," I repeated. "Nothing more."

Enzo held his hands up. "Dude, I didn't mean anything by it."

Harrison let go and dropped his arm around my waist. He didn't apologize, and I had a feeling it was because he didn't think he'd done anything wrong. I only had time to flash Enzo a brief smile and a wave before Harrison hustled me towards the door. As he pushed it open for me, he lowered his head and confirmed my suspicions—he wasn't the least bit sorry. "Nobody touches what's mine, baby doll. And you're very much mine."

Chapter 5
Harrison

I spent the majority of the night in my hotel room tossing and turning. Bunny and Stanley had decided to follow tradition and spend the night before their wedding apart. Leaving without kissing my girl goodnight was one of the hardest things I've ever done. At least, I'd thought so at the time. I soon discovered that I wouldn't sleep well without her near.

What if that little punk tried to climb into her room? Bunny wouldn't be any kind of help. She'd probably unlock the window and lower a rope. I growled at nobody in particular, the thought irritating the shit out of me.

Finally, I couldn't take it any longer. I climbed out of bed and threw on a black T-shirt and basketball shorts in the same color. After grabbing my keys and wallet, I made my way to the parking lot and drove off. I parked a couple of houses down and walked the rest of the way to Maggie's house. Crossing the lawn, I looked up to the window where I knew her room was located.

I was in great shape, but I still wasn't a teenager anymore, so even if this was a movie scene with the perfect tree for me to climb, I'd probably fall and break my neck.

Silently, I creeped around to the backyard and tested the sliding door into my room. I didn't know whether to be grateful or furious that it was unlocked. It glided open and I went in, closing it behind me. Then, with the experience of years of staying silent and invisible in order to photograph animals and other skittish subjects, I made my way upstairs to Maggie.

Her door was cracked open and I pushed it further so I could step inside. After closing it behind me, I twisted the lock slowly so it wouldn't click. Walking over to her bed, I drank in the sight of my sweet girl sleeping, curled around her pillow, and breathing evenly. She looked like an angel with her silvery hair spread across the pillow, her plump lips slightly parted, and her pale skin luminescent in the glow from the night sky.

Tonight, she was wearing a short, cotton nightgown with spaghetti straps that showed off her beautiful collarbone and shoulder, and exposed a great deal of her long, gorgeous legs. As my erection swelled painfully, I vaguely wondered if I would always be this affected by her. I hoped so.

Gently, I pushed her gown up and hooked my fingers into the waistband of her panties. I pulled them down and stuffed them in my pocket, then pushed the gown higher until it was above her breasts. Holy fuck. Those were the most incredible tits I had ever seen.

Maggie was a heavy sleeper, but she finally stirred as I pulled her pajamas completely off. "Harrison?" she asked sleepily.

"You better not have been expecting to wake up and find someone else undressing you, baby doll." I grunted as I stood up and whipped my shirt off. I left my shorts on, very aware of my limits. Maggie was all creamy skin and lush curves, and I could have stood there and stared at her all night. But, I craved the feel of her against me.

"What are you doing here?"

I didn't answer, just slipped into her bed and adjusted her so we were spooning. When her naked back pressed to my chest, our skin sizzled. My hard on was nestled in the crack of her ass, one arm under her head, the other cupping her breast. She wiggled and I gave it a squeeze. "Quit squirming and go to sleep, baby doll." She sighed in disappointment and I buried my smile in her hair. "I promise to take care of you tomorrow night, sweet Maggie. For now, I just want to hold you."

She sighed again, but this time, it had an air of contentment. I kissed her temple and tucked her in a little closer before finally falling asleep.

The best light for photographs is usually dawn and dusk. After spending so many years waking early for the good shots, my internal clock always woke me as the sun started to rise.

At some point in the night, Maggie had turned over and snuggled deep into my embrace, her face buried in my chest. Her soft breaths heated my skin and one of her legs was haphazardly thrown on both of mine. It was sexy as hell, but her mother would be up in a few hours and my brother would be knocking on my hotel room door.

I lifted her face with a finger under her chin and kissed her softly. "I have to go, baby doll." She grumbled and tried to burrow in further. She was so fucking cute, it spread warmth through my blood. I repeated the previous action. "Wake up for just a minute, Maggie."

Her eyelids fluttered and soon I was looking down into her sky blue eyes, still cloudy with sleep. "Don't go," she begged. It almost broke my resolve, but I held strong.

"I think we should talk and have some time to ourselves before we tell anyone about us, don't you agree?" She nodded reluctantly. I rewarded her acceptance with a brush of my lips over hers. "Then I should go before I'm discovered in your room." Her bottom lip turned out in a pout and I leaned down to nibble on it, making her giggle.

"Get some more sleep, baby doll. I'll see you down the aisle." I started to slip out of bed, then paused and turned back to her. "It'll be good practice." Her eyes widened and her cheeks turned bright pink, but a small smile graced her lips.

Getting out of bed, I grabbed my shirt and put it on, then headed for her door. I had just grabbed the handle when I heard her hiss my name. I halted and twisted my head to look at her over my shoulder. She'd put her nightgown back on and was glaring at me. "Did you take my underwear again?"

I smirked and left the room as silently as I'd entered. Once I was back at the hotel, I laid down to try and rest for a couple more hours. It was a fruitless endeavor because every time I closed my eyes all I could see was Maggie's naked body. Fuck. That girl could be a fucking porn star with that body, those lips . . . not that anyone but me would ever see her assets.

I gave up after a while and got up to take a long, hot shower. After getting ready, I sat down to go through shots from my last assignment. When Stanley showed up, I'd just finished writing my article and had sent it and the photos I'd chosen to my editor. I'd also sent a quick note about having a chat about my next few assignments.

Stanley and I ordered room service and shot the shit for an hour or so. It had been a really long time since we'd been able to just sit down and visit like that.

"You seem really happy," I observed.

He grinned almost dreamily . . . a look I had rarely, if ever, seen on him. "I am. Bunny is—she's—I don't even know how to describe it. She's amazing." He leaned back in his chair and relaxed. "And Maggie. I couldn't have asked for a better step-daughter. From the first moment she realized how much I loved her mother, she's been completely supportive of our relationship. She's bright, mature, smart, and such a joy to be around."

I listened silently, afraid that if I commented, if only to agree, that he would hear the truth of my feelings for Maggie in my voice.

"She's taken care of Bunny for so long," he continued. "I'm hoping now that I'm here to take over that task, she'll take the opportunity to just be a kid for a while."

I grunted and he seemed to take it as an agreement. At eleven o'clock, we gathered our things and left the hotel for the church. The ceremony was set to start at noon, so we weren't surprised to see several cars already in the lot. The girls would have gotten there a while ago to start getting ready.

We took our places at the alter at ten till as the last of the guests were seated. Another few minutes went by and then a woman seated at a black grand piano began to play the sweet, joyful tune of *Music Box Dancer*. The back door opened and Maggie stepped into the room, causing all of the air in my lungs to rush out.

She was dressed in a strapless lavender gown. The corset top had gathered material to her waist where it smoothed and flared out, falling to her feet. Her blonde curls were swept up behind her head and her blue eyes sparkled as she caught my eye and smiled.

She slowly moved down the aisle and as she neared, her gaze lowered so she wasn't blatantly staring at me. I wanted to lift her head back up so I could still see her beautiful eyes, but I dutifully stayed in my spot. As soon as she took her place, the music switched to a cello and piano rendition of *My Love* by Paul McCartney.

I assumed Bunny had entered and was making her way towards Stanley, but all I could see was Maggie. I pictured her dress in white and the two of us standing alone in front of the arch where Stanley and Bunny met to make their vows.

The ceremony was over before I'd even realized it had begun. I gave Stanley a typical guy hug, pounding him on the back. "Congratulations, brother." He grinned and started to turn to his bride, but stopped and looked at me.

"Your turn, Harrison," he said.

I laughed and shook my head airily. "I'll work on that." My tone had a sarcastic edge to it, but as soon as his back was turned, my attention diverted to Maggie. He had no idea that work was already in progress. I'd found the one for me and I wasn't going to wait to officially make her mine.

Chapter 6
Maggie

The wedding reception was gorgeous. Everything was exactly as my mom and Stanley, my step-dad now, had wanted things. It was perfect... except for one small problem. A five-foot-four irritation, dressed in a slutty red dress which was completely inappropriate for a wedding unless you were in Vegas, who refused to go away.

"Are you sure you don't want to dance?" Cynthia, one of Stanley's employees, asked Harrison. Yet again. *For about the millionth time.*

He didn't even glance up at her as he answered this time around, keeping his eyes focused on my face instead. His frustration with the situation was clear in his eyes, and it was the only thing that was keeping me from acting like a jealous bitch. "I'm happy right where I am. If you'll excuse us, Maggie and I were in the middle of a conversation when you interrupted us."

The woman flashed me a condescending smile and leaned lower, making sure her ample cleavage was on display. "I'm sure little Maggie will be fine on her own. Your brother couldn't have possibly expected a man like you to spend all your time with his new daughter tonight."

Harrison's hand dropped onto my upper thigh, holding me in place when I would have shoved my chair back to confront her myself. He gave me a small shake of his head before turning to face Cynthia. "I was trying to be polite since this is my brother's wedding reception, and I don't want to cause a scene. But apparently subtle doesn't work with you, so it looks like I'm going to have to go with the direct approach instead. I'm more than sure that I have no interest in dancing with you tonight. Or any night for that matter. It wasn't the first time you asked me, and I sure as shit am not going to change my mind because you're displaying how much of a bitch you can be when confronted with a much prettier and younger woman than you."

"I—" she gasped, straightening up and putting one hand to her chest as her cheeks filled with an embarrassed flush.

"I don't know if you've been drinking or if you're just incredibly stupid, but behavior like this at your boss's wedding isn't smart. My advice to you is to head home before you get yourself into the kind of trouble which will have long-lasting consequences."

The fresh color in her cheeks quickly drained out, leaving her pale and trembling before us. I probably should have felt bad for her, but I didn't. I was too busy trying to stop myself from grabbing Harrison and giving him a big kiss for how he'd handled her. As she walked away from us—finally—I leaned over to whisper in his ear, "Please tell me we can get out of here and head home now."

"No"—my heart fell, only to rise back up right again as he continued—"but we can head to my hotel room."

"Your hotel room, huh?"

"Yeah," he breathed out. "The first time I take you isn't going to be in your room, in the home you share with your mother and my brother. It's going to be in a bed I've provided for you, as I make you a woman. My woman."

"Now, please," I whimpered.

"Let me go tell Stanley and your mom that we're leaving, and that we'll meet them for brunch tomorrow before they head to the airport. That way, if we bump into them in the morning, they won't wonder what we're doing at the hotel."

"But I don't have a change of clothes with me, except for what I was wearing this morning."

"No worries, baby doll," he reassured me. "I grabbed you a few things when I snuck out of your house this morning."

We gathered up my purse and wrap, and headed over to my mom and Stanley to say our goodbyes.

"Are you sure you'll be okay tonight?" my mom asked, looking worried. "Maybe we should just stay at the house with you one more night."

She turned to look at Stanley, and he nodded in agreement. "Whatever you want, Bunny."

"No, really," I disagreed. "You're not going to change your wedding night plans for me. I'm eighteen, and I'm not even going to be alone."

"Exactly. She'll be with me from now on, and I promise to take very good care of her," Harrison added.

Neither my mom or Stanley caught the hidden meaning behind his words, but I did. It sounded like a promise to me, as he told them I was going to be with him from now on. He wasn't just talking about the time they'd be gone on their honeymoon, but more than that. It almost sounded like he meant forever, and I hoped it wasn't just my naiveté making me think that, since I fully intended to give him my virginity tonight. I couldn't picture him taking it and then leaving me behind when he left, but I could easily picture me going with him after graduation. But, would he be willing to wait the three months? It was something that had been nagging at me, but I'd tried hard to ignore it.

We were both quiet as we left the ballroom where the reception was held and got in the elevator. We weren't alone, and I was nervous someone was going to ask why I was going up to his room with him. I was thinking about what our cover story would be—that he needed to grab his things before taking me home—as we got off and walked to his room. When the door shut behind us, I heaved a deep sigh of relief knowing we were finally alone. Just the two of us. In a hotel room with a huge, king-sized bed.

"Oh, my," I breathed out, catching sight of the rose petals strewn on the floor and across the comforter. There was soft music playing and the lights were turned down low. Off to the side of the bed, there was a tray of chocolate covered strawberries on the table with a bucket of ice that had an open bottle of champagne sticking out of it. "You did all of this? For me?"

"Only for you, baby doll." There was no doubting the honesty blazing from his eyes. "It's your first time, and I wanted it to be special."

"Wow," I sighed.

"You want a glass of champagne?"

"I thought you were saving that for when you took me to France?" I teased.

"This is American champagne. I'll introduce you to the French kind after graduation."

"How about we save the American kind for after."

He cocked his head and raised his eyebrows. "After what?"

"After you make me yours."

That was all it took for his control to snap. He began stripping me out of my clothes, and soon I was standing before him completely naked. I didn't have time to feel awkward or shy because I was completely focused on him while he practically tore his tuxedo from his body. Then he shoved his boxers down his legs, and I got my first view of his cock. He was already erect, and it was way bigger than I expected, even after rubbing against it the other night.

"You sure it's going to fit?" I blushed as soon as the words left my mouth of their own accord.

He stalked towards me, staring down into my eyes when his body was only inches away from mine. "Trust me, baby doll."

"I do trust you."

His heated gaze flared even brighter and then he swept me up in his arms and dropped me onto the mattress. "I'll do everything in my power to make sure you never regret giving me the gift of your trust."

Excitement flared through me, and I wiggled with anticipation under him. I trailed my hands along his skin as he moved over me to settle between my legs with his forearms braced on either side of my body. His head bent low and his mouth went to my breasts, hot and hungry. I gasped loudly and ran my fingers through his hair. He tongued my nipples into hard peaks before trailing lower. Over my belly, circling my belly button before flicking down to just above my clit.

My nails dug into his shoulders as he teased me. "Are you wet for me, baby doll?" he rasped out.

"Yes," I whimpered, levering my hips up to get closer to his mouth.

"I think I'll taste you and find out for myself."

His mouth dipped, stroking against my clit and making my breath shudder out of me on a long moan. He murmured something soothing against my skin and licked me harder. Long, deep swipes of his tongue, from my clit down to my entrance. He licked and sucked at me until I couldn't take it anymore. Until I arched into his mouth as I shattered with a shout.

His finger slid into me, prolonging my orgasm as he stroked me higher and higher. As I clenched against him, he added another, stretching me while I twisted and turned underneath his body. Then he moved over me, his big body sliding over mine. With his cock pressed against my core, he paused.

"You ready for this, baby doll?"

"More than ready." I slid my palms down his back until they reached his ass. "I want you so much, Harrison. Take me."

"Mine," he growled, sinking to the hilt with one powerful thrust.

I tensed beneath him, shocked by the searing pain and how stretched I felt with him inside me. I knew it was going to hurt, but I'd never expected it to feel quite like this. Harrison held his lower body still while he kissed the tears from the corner of my eyes. "You're so beautiful," he whispered as he kissed his way to my ear.

"Amazing." He trailed down my jaw.

"Perfect." His lips hovered over mine before he claimed them in a passionate kiss.

By the time he lifted his head again, the pain was gone and I was writhing underneath him, trying to get him to move. "Please," I whimpered.

It must have been the sign he was looking for because he began to pump furiously between my legs. I wrapped my arms around his neck, holding on tight, crying out with each thrust. The feel of his cock, dragging along my sensitive walls, brought me to another shattering orgasm in minutes and I screamed his name. Harrison followed close behind, groaning my name as he came. His body quaked against mine, and I'd never felt closer to anyone else than I did in that moment. He hadn't just made me his tonight. He'd become mine as well.

Chapter 7
Harrison

Casual hookups had never been my thing, so I'd spent years waking up alone in hotel rooms and various other random places, depending on the assignment. After waking up with Maggie in my arms, I knew I'd never be able to go back to that. The last few nights had been the best sleep I'd ever gotten, even if it was only for a few hours. Maggie soothed my soul; she gave me peace and contentment. But, what was most surprising to me, when I was with her, I no longer felt the restlessness that had fueled my need to globetrot.

Don't get me wrong, I would always love to travel and I was beyond excited to take Maggie everywhere she wanted to go. But, my worry that staying in one place, particularly this small town while she finished school, was gone. I would be content anywhere as long as I had her with me.

I eased back and leaned up on my elbow to watch Maggie sleep. Her body was turned towards mine. She seemed to like to virtually crawl inside me as she slept. It was so fucking adorable and I had not one complaint about it. Her silvery hair streamed behind her on the pillow and her kiss-swollen lips were turned up in a tiny smile. She was so beautiful, inside and out. Obviously, I felt a jolt of lust, but there was also a warmth that bloomed in my chest and spread throughout my body.

Love at first sight was something I used to laugh about. I believed it was a made up excuse by hopeless romantics who got laid on the first date. I was now eating every joke I had ever made about it. Maggie had stolen my heart from the very first moment we met. I'd fallen fast and hard when I looked into her clear blue eyes. She owned me. And I'd never been happier about anything in my whole life than belonging to Magnolia Bloom.

I glanced at the clock on the desk across the room and saw that it was just before nine. We were meeting her parents for brunch at ten. I hated to wake her, I'd taken her three times the night before and I knew she was exhausted. She was going to be sore and while I hated to think of her in pain, a little part of me was cheering at the thought of her being reminded that she was mine every time she moved.

Leaning down, I brushed my lips softly over hers, then kissed the tip of her nose. "Time to get up, baby doll," I murmured in her ear. As was her habit, she grumbled something unintelligible and scooted closer to burrow into my chest. My chuckle turned into a groan when her lips brushed my nipple as she turned her head to peer up at me.

Her leg was thrown over mine and she was so close that when my morning wood began to swell even more, it pressed right into her center. She was clearly aroused because her cream coated my cock. Her pink little tongue darted out and licked my nipple.

"Fuck!" I hissed as I flipped her onto her back. All of my good intentions were shot to hell as I settled over her. "You're already going to be sore, Maggie," I grunted. "I shouldn't fuck you again until you've had a chance to heal." I dropped my forehead to rest in the valley between her breasts, telling myself to move, to stop.

Her hands plunged into my hair and she lifted my head to press her lips to mine. *Fuck it.* I rubbed my shaft over her pussy, getting it nice and slick. She mewled and the sound was like a strike of lightening, sending a zing of electricity straight to my dick. I shifted my hips so that my tip was at her entrance and circled it a few times, making sure to glide over her clit.

"Please," she whimpered.

"What do you want, sweet Maggie?" I rasped, circling my hips once more.

"Inside." She was panting, and the word came out on a quick exhale.

I slammed my mouth down over hers as I cautiously pushed inside her. She was so wet that I easily slid right in, only stopping when I was balls deep. "Oh fuck, yeah," I sighed. "This has to be what heaven is like." Then I began to move, slowly at first, then gaining speed. Maggie's head fell back onto her pillow, her hips bucking up to meet my every thrust.

I grabbed one of her legs and threw it over my shoulder, changing the angle so I hit just the right spot.

"Yes! Yes!" she cried out, each time I bottomed out inside her. Last night, I'd encouraged her to let loose, to be as loud and vocal as she wanted. It was sexy as hell and I didn't give a fuck if it could be heard in the room next door.

Grabbing her ass, I raised it up and got to my knees. I lifted her other leg to join the first, both on one shoulder, and it tightened her pussy around my cock. "Fuck, your pussy is squeezing me so tight." With one hand still supporting her bottom, my other traveled up her damp skin to her large, bouncing tits. I pinched the nipples, twisting and plucking, escalating her cries.

When she was just about to break, I shifted one leg to my other shoulder so she was open to me and I could watch myself sink inside her. It was the most erotic sight I'd ever seen and I was seconds from exploding.

"Fuck, yes. So good. I love seeing my cock disappear inside you. So fucking wet," I ground out through clenched teeth. "Your pussy is gorgeous, baby doll. And all mine." I growled the last part, feeling an almost feral possessiveness.

My fingers found her swollen little clit and I pinched it hard. "Come for me, sweet Maggie."

The moment her walls clamped down on my cock, signaling her orgasm, mine burst from me as well. I buried myself so deep, we were fused together into one entity. We didn't exist without each other. Come poured into her in hot spurts and like the last three times, I spent half a second wondering if I should have used a condom.

Then the knowledge that I was leaving something of myself behind, that Maggie would have me inside her all day, branding her as mine, eclipsed any other thought.

When I was empty and completely sated, I pulled out and dropped down beside her, tugging her into my arms. Our chests were heaving with exertion, our hearts racing, and I was utterly content. "Being with you gets better every time, baby doll," I murmured before placing a kiss on her temple. "I'd love to do nothing more than spend all day in this bed making love to you."

"Sounds like a plan," she answered with a yawn.

I grinned and kissed her head again. "But"—I laughed at her cute little growl— "we have brunch with Bunny and Stanley in about half an hour."

Maggie shot up in bed, almost knocking her head on my chin. "Oh, crap. I have to shower! I can't face my mom and step-dad smelling like sex!" she screeched as she scooted off the bed and raced to the bathroom. "They won't know, right?" she called frantically. "I mean, how could they tell? It's not like I have 'Harrison popped my cherry and screwed me four times' tattooed on my forehead." She continued rambling as I joined her in the shower.

"A tattoo that warns everyone you're mine isn't a bad idea," I teased. "Maybe not those exact words..."

She glared at me as she scrubbed her body with soap and I chuckled. My eyes were drawn to her hands as they moved and I grabbed the body wash from her to take over the job. Cupping her full tits, I made sure they were extremely clean, then I dragged my hands over the rest of her, paying special attention to the area between her legs.

She tried to hide it, but I caught the tiny hiss of pain she emitted as I gently cleansed her pussy. I was such an ass for fucking her so many times right after taking her virginity. I just couldn't seem to stop thinking with my dick when she was naked and pressed against me. Go figure.

We finished up in the shower and quickly dressed. I was extra careful when zipping my shorts because I'd left the shower harder than when I'd entered. I put on a casual, button-down shirt that hung long enough to hide my aroused state and rolled up the sleeves.

It was five 'til when Maggie stepped out of the bathroom in the sundress and sandals I'd brought her and declared herself ready to go. Thankfully, we still managed to beat Stanley and Bunny to the hotel restaurant. I wasn't going to wait long before opening declaring Maggie as mine, but I didn't want anything to spoil their honeymoon, so we kept it our secret for the moment.

They arrived shortly after us and the waitress took our orders before leaving us alone. The tall, skinny brunette had smiled seductively at me and since I couldn't pull Maggie into my side as a show that I was taken, I simply frowned sternly at her until she avoided my gaze.

"Magnolia," Bunny began with a smile. "I've left your school and activity schedule on the kitchen counter for Harrison. So no skipping out just because you think he won't know the difference." Maggie returned her mother's smile, but I didn't miss the slight eye roll that went with it and I cough-laughed into my napkin.

"I've never skipped before and I hadn't planned on starting a few months before graduation," she said without snark, simply stating fact.

Stanley beamed at her and nodded his head proudly. "Magnolia is an excellent student," he boasted to me.

The conversation evolved from Maggie's accomplishments to talk of her parents' honeymoon, and then to last minute instructions for her while they were gone. I could see how much it frustrated Maggie that they treated her like a child. But, she handled it like the amazing woman I knew she was.

We saw them off and then went back into the hotel to gather our things and check out. Maggie was quiet throughout and on the drive back to her house. I reached across and laced our fingers together, setting them on her thigh.

"What's on your mind, baby doll?"

She sighed and stared out her window. "What if they won't accept us as a couple?" she asked worriedly. "I've been as responsible as an adult for more than half of my life and now that I'm actually one legally, they treat me like I'm twelve."

I squeezed her hand and brought it to my lips for a kiss. "If they don't take it well at first, they'll come around eventually," I assured her.

We pulled into the driveway and I put the car in park before turning to face her. I unbuckled her and lifted her over to straddle my lap. I kissed her forehead, nose, and lips.

"I don't care if they don't. I choose you, Harrison," she said almost shyly. "If you want me." She added the last part as pinked tinged her cheeks.

Smiling tenderly, I brushed her hair away from her face. "Of course I want you. I love you, baby doll. Once they see that, I have no doubt they'll be okay with us."

Maggie's eyes widened to the size of saucers and her jaw dropped. I closed it gently and kissed her, pouring all of my love into it. When we came up for air, I rested my forehead against hers.

"Tell me, Maggie," I demanded, keeping my tone soft so I didn't sound harsh. I leaned back and she still looked a little shell-shocked. "Say it."

She shook her head a little, as if to shake away clutter in her mind. "I love you, too."

Inside my head, a caveman was beating on his chest and shouted out that his woman loved him. However, what I actually said was, "Good girl." Then I kissed her.

Chapter 8
Maggie

"Honey, I'm home!" I called out as I walked through the front door of my house. I'd always loved the home I shared with my mom, but I'd found a new appreciation for sharing space with Harrison over the last eight days. I'd kind of expected it to be awkward since I'd never even had a boyfriend before. Moving from a complete lack of a love life to basically living with my boyfriend—for a lack of a better term since in no way, shape, or form was Harrison a boy—should have been a major adjustment. But it really hadn't been, at least not in a negative way. Harrison and I just seemed to fit together.

"Hey, baby doll," he mumbled distractedly. He was sprawled out on the couch in the living room with his laptop perched on his knees. His hair was mussed, like he'd been running his fingers through it, and he was dressed in a dark T-shirt and athletic shorts. It was his usual choice when he was hanging around the house, at least until he stripped out of them because he much preferred being naked in bed with me. And on the couch. In the kitchen. Pretty much anywhere and everywhere.

Naked sexy time was a regular pastime for us, but I couldn't help wondering what was going to happen when my mom and Stanley returned from their honeymoon. Their trip was already more than half-way over, which meant my alone time with Harrison was flying by in a blink of an eye. We only had six days left.

"How was school?"

"Same old, same old," I answered, bending low to give him a quick kiss on the lips. When I tried to lift back up, he shifted his laptop onto the cushion next to him and pulled me onto his lap.

"You didn't really think I was going to let you get away from me that easily, did you?"

"Hmmm," I hummed against his lips. "You didn't really think I was trying to get away from you, did you?"

I felt his deep chuckle as it rumbled up his chest, and then his lips claimed mine for a deep, wet kiss. His tongue swept in my mouth to tangle with mine as his fingers slid up my neck to the base of my skull to hold me in place as he plundered my mouth.

"Well played, baby doll," he rasped when he lifted his head. "Do you have a lot of homework to do tonight?"

"Not much. I did most of it while I was there." It's what I'd done all of last week, too. I didn't want to waste any time while I was home with Harrison. So I finished it up while I was already away from him.

"You sure that's cool with your teachers?"

"Yeah, no worries. They all love me."

"Oh, they do, do they?" he growled, flipping me over until my back was on the cushions and he hovered over me. "Do I need to visit your school to make sure none of these teachers are guys who're getting the wrong idea about my woman?"

"Nope." I made a popping sound on the 'P.'

"Good, cause I'd hate to have to kick some ass at your school."

His possessive caveman act shouldn't have turned me on, but it did. Then again, it wasn't like I could point any fingers in his direction about it since I was just as bad whenever women flirted with him right in front of me, which happened way too often for my liking. Keeping our relationship under wraps until my mom and Stanley got home was starting to drive me crazy. As scared as I was about how they'd react, I'd reached the point where I was ready to shout about us from the rooftops.

Sliding my palms down his side, I jabbed my fingers into his waist and tickled him. He'd mentioned he had one place where he was ticklish, but I hadn't managed to find it yet.

"Good try, but that's not it," he laughed.

"I'm going to find it sooner or later," I grumbled.

"I'm sure you are, since you've got a lifetime to look for it."

I beamed up at him, my heart lifting at how open he was about his feelings with me. How he always talked as though we'd be together forever. "I love you."

"Love you, too, baby doll."

His stomach growled, ruining our romantic moment.

"Didn't you eat anything while I was gone?"

He levered off me, reaching a hand down to pull me to my feet too. "Shit, I totally forgot. I was wrapped up in work stuff and didn't even realize what time it was until you got home."

"I guess it's a good thing I put my famous chicken taco recipe in the crockpot before I left this morning. It's amazing what you can do with chicken breasts, a drizzle of oil, and salsa in one of those things." As we walked into the kitchen, I lifted my nose and sniffed. "Although, I have to admit that I'm worried about your sense of smell. How could you have forgotten to eat with all this yumminess in the air?"

"That's a damn good question," he chuckled, following behind me to lean over my shoulder and peer into the crockpot when I lifted the lid. "I spent most of the morning reading through assignment proposals from my editor. I narrowed it down to a couple that sounded the most promising and spent the next couple hours doing some research on them."

"What kind of assignments?" I tried asking it as nonchalantly as possible, but my voice wavered at the end. Harrison's work usually took him all across the globe, but I was stuck here until graduation. The thought of being separated by so many miles this early in our relationship scared the crap out of me.

He nuzzled his chin in the crook of my neck, his breath hot against my skin. "What do you think about alligators?"

"I try not to think about them usually." I tilted my head to smile up at him. "Even though that's hard to do when I spot one at least once a month or so."

"But they don't completely freak you out, right?"

"Nah, I'm a Florida girl after all."

"It's a good thing my girl grew up in Florida because one of the assignments my editor offered me involves a short trip to the Everglades, and I was hoping you'd want to come with me."

"Really?" I squealed, turning in his arms.

"Of course, really, silly girl." He tweaked my nose. "I told him I was unavailable for anything outside of the country for the next three months. Several of the proposals he sent would work, but the Everglades one is the closest to home so it's the one I told him I'd take."

"Closest to home," I echoed in a breathy voice.

"Yeah, I figure we can look for apartments over the next couple days."

"Apartments. Here?"

"Of course, baby doll. Where else? My home is wherever you are."

While he continued to ramble on, as though he hadn't just said something earth-shattering, I dropped the lid back on the crockpot and turned the setting down to warm. Then I turned around in Harrison's arms so we could have this talk face-to-face.

"It shouldn't be too hard to pick one that'll work for us until graduation. My lease isn't up on my place in Miami, but that's not a big deal. It won't matter if I leave it empty for a while. As soon as we find a place here, I'll arrange for the movers to box all my stuff up and get it to the new house. That way, everything will be set before Stanley and Bunny make it back into town on Sunday."

"Harrison," I interrupted softly. "Are you asking me to move in with you?"

"Fuck, no, baby doll," he breathed against my lips as he lifted me up, and I wrapped my legs around his waist. "There's no asking involved. I'm *telling* you we're getting an apartment together. There's no way in hell you and I can live here with Stanley and Bunny."

My heart stuttered a little. "Because they aren't going to approve of us as a couple?"

"No, because you're a screamer," he corrected. "And we aren't going to spend the next few months having quiet sex just because we don't want them to hear how wild I make you. Not when I love to hear your voice ringing in my ears when you come. I'm not giving that up for anybody."

"I'm not that loud," I pouted as a wild blush stole across my cheeks.

"Yes, you are," he purred.

"Oh yeah?" I huffed. "Prove it."

"Game on," he growled.

It was a game he won. Repeatedly. After the third screaming orgasm, he made me agree to move in with him. What I didn't say was that I would have said yes from that start. I didn't need any convincing, but I sure as heck wasn't going to argue with his method of persuasion.

Harrison

My phone beeped and I flipped my shades up so I could see the screen in the bright sun. I smiled at the message. I'd just gotten the confirmation I'd been waiting for. Maggie would be out of school any minute and I was leaning against my car in the parking lot, waiting for her.

Putting my phone back in my pocket, I squinted at the front door before remembering to pull my sunglasses off my head to cover my eyes. The entrance banged open and students piled out, some laughing and walking casually, others running towards busses, but I didn't really see any of them.

The love of my life stepped outside, her head bowed as she typed something on her phone. Mine pinged and I retrieved it with a chuckle.

Baby doll: *On my way home. Want anything?*

Me: *I want many things from you, babe. But, let's start with a hello kiss.*

Her lips tipped up in a sweet smile when she stopped to read my reply.

Baby doll: *I can't wait.*

I grinned.

Me: *Then don't. How about right now? And, did I mention that you look fucking edible in that dress?*

Maggie's head flew up and her eyes scanned the parking lot eagerly until they landed on me. Her smile grew to epic proportions and she immediately started to run my way.

As she got closer, her eyes darted around and she slowed, coming to a stop about a foot in front of me. I narrowed my eyes and frowned.

She looked around again and sighed. "I guess it will have to wait."

"Fuck that," I growled as I grabbed her hips and yanked her against me. I lowered my head and crushed my mouth down over hers. My hands bunched the material of her simple, pink summer dress and my tongue plundered her mouth. I didn't stop devouring her until she was clinging to me and kissing me back with equal enthusiasm.

"You're more delicious every time I taste you, baby doll."

Her cheeks turned pink but she grinned up at me, her eyes squinting in the rays of the sun. I pulled off my aviators and set them on her nose. They were a little too big for her face, but she looked damn cute.

"I thought we were still hiding our relationship," she said breathlessly.

I shook my head, then kissed the tip of her nose. "You're done with school for the week and Stanley and Bunny will be home in two days. No one is going to out us before we have a chance to tell them. I doubt anyone even knows who I am anyway."

She shrugged, her smile still firmly in place. "Okay." Her hands dove into my hair and she tugged my head down for another soul deep kiss. "I love you," she whispered when she pulled away.

"Love you, too, baby doll. Now, let's go. I have a surprise for you."

I helped her into my sporty red car and buckled her up. After kissing her quickly once more, I shut her door and jogged around to the driver's side. I got settled and then followed the line of cars out of the parking lot.

We drove for about ten minutes before I turned down a tree lined street with small houses on either side. Maggie stared through the window, watching the scenery without comment. Another few minutes and I pulled into the driveway of a light blue, cottage style house, the color almost matching Maggie's eyes.

She looked at me with confusion. "Why are we here?"

I winked at her, but exited the car without answering. Going around, I helped her out and took her hand, then led her to the front door. Pulling out the key, I ignored her gasp as I inserted it into the lock and twisted.

We stepped inside and I shut the door before spinning her around and backing her into it. I palmed her ass and lifted her so her legs wrapped around my waist. She glanced around wildly and started to protest, but I silenced her by sealing my mouth over hers. It didn't take long to drive her so wild that she forgot all about where we were.

I had learned all about Maggie's spectacular body and I knew how to push her over the edge quickly. With my fingers in her pussy and my tongue in her mouth, I drove her to a screaming orgasm. It was hot as fuck and a little come spurted from my steely shaft. I buried my face in her neck, and using every technique in the figurative book, I calmed myself and kept from giving in to the orgasm I was on the edge of.

"I love hearing the sounds of your ecstasy, baby doll," I mumbled, and kissed her neck. "It occurred to me that if we lived in an apartment, we'd have to be conscious of neighbors." Lifting my head, I stared into her wide curious eyes. "Since I'm not about to give that up, I decided to do some digging. With a little help from a friend, I discovered that the owner of this house is about to put it on the market, but they're waiting a few months for some reason. I contacted him about temporarily renting it and it turns out, he's a fan. He offered for us to stay here until you graduate if I photograph a spread for him. It's even furnished, so I'll put my stuff in storage for now."

As I spoke, Maggie's face began to light up and when I was done with my little speech, she was absolutely glowing with excitement. "This is ours?" she gasped.

I laughed. "Until you graduate, yes. Then we'll figure out where we want to call home."

"Harrison!" she screeched happily. "This is amazing! Show me around!"

It was impossible not to be happy around my girl, but when she was overflowing with joy, it was like being in paradise. I set her down and she righted her clothing before grabbing my hand. We took a tour of the small, one bedroom, one bath house, which only took about ten minutes.

"I love it," she announced once we'd returned to the front room. "But not because it's an adorable house, which it is. But, because it's ours. Just you and me."

Maggie sighed and laid her head on my shoulder. I had one hand on the steering wheel and the other on her thigh as I drove us home from Miami.

"This was the best weekend ever," she said dreamily. I kept my eyes on the road, but managed to twist my head enough to kiss her forehead. After I'd shown her the house, I'd taken off for the city, having already packed us a bag and thrown it in my trunk. We went to a delicious little Cuban place near my apartment and I took her dancing. Afterwards, we spent the night making love at my place.

I hated to go back to her house because Stanley and Bunny would be back tomorrow and it would burst the little bubble we'd been living in. At the same time, I was eager to get things out in the open and start living the rest of my life with my Maggie.

"I'm glad you had such a great time, baby doll. We'll have to make dinner and dancing—followed by a marathon fucking session—a regular occurrence."

She giggled and kissed my chin. After a few minutes of silence, I noticed the mood in the car becoming thick and a little dark. "What's wrong, baby doll?" I asked concernedly.

Another little sigh escaped, but this time it didn't hold the same happiness as before. "I'm nervous about tomorrow," she admitted morosely. "I don't want Stanley or my mom to be upset, I want them to be happy for us."

She finished as I glided to a stop on the curb in front of her house. I lifted her face to mine and sweetly kissed her lips. "Do you love me?" I asked. She nodded without hesitation. "And, you know I love you, right?" She smiled and nodded again.

"Then there's nothing else to worry about because we have each other. Yeah, maybe Stanley and Bunny will be pissed when they first find out about us being a couple. However, I believe they will come to our way of thinking once they realize how much we love each other."

"I don't know if I believe you one hundred percent, but you make me feel a heck of a lot better," she teased.

I took her face in my hands and kissed the ever-loving fuck out of her, then mumbled against her lips. "Later, I'm going to make you feel so much more," I promised gruffly.

"Later?" she asked with a small pout.

I laughed. "Damn you're cute, baby doll. Yeah, we've got some things to do, then I promise we'll go to bed early and I'll give you all the feels."

"Hmmm," she hummed. "Those are some lofty goals, Harrison." She winked and got out of the car. *Fucking adorable.*

We made arrangements to have some of my stuff shipped to our house and the rest put away. Then we took a load of Maggie's things to our place since I was adamant that we'd be sleeping there starting tomorrow night. I had some work to do and got most of it finished while she finished her school work and then made dinner.

I ended up eating a good portion of it off of her naked body before scooping her up and stalking to my bedroom. Laying her down gently on the bed, my gaze swept over her. "Every night, I think I couldn't possibly love you more, then the morning comes and I realize that I was wrong. You get more beautiful, more precious to me, more loveable every damn day, baby doll."

A tear leaked from the corner of her eye and I started to panic. Why the fuck was she crying? Then she smiled, lighting up the room like she was the surface of the sun. She held her arms out to me.

"About those feels..."

Chapter 10
Maggie

Looking around my bedroom—or my old room I guessed I should call it since my new home was with Harrison—I was filled with an odd mixture of emotions. Mainly it was excitement about what the future would bring after graduation. There was also a huge dose of anxiety over how my mom and Stanley were going to react to the news of our relationship. Add to that some sentimentality over leaving the only home I'd ever known, and I was a jumbled mess of nerves.

"You look sad," Harrison breathed into my ear, after coming up behind me and wrapping his arms around my body to pull me into his chest.

"Not sad, just a little moody," I corrected, scanning the room. It mostly looked the same, except my bookshelf was empty because we'd already brought all my books to the house. A quick peek into the dresser and closet would show they were almost empty since we'd taken most of my clothes over, too. "It's hard to believe I'm leaving, that's all."

He turned me in his arms and looked down at me, his light brown eyes filled with concern. "If you aren't ready to move into the rental house yet, just say the word and we'll stay here a little longer. It'll feel a little odd, living under the same roof with your mom and my brother, but I'll deal with it. The only thing that's important is your happiness."

I promptly burst into tears and buried my face into his chest.

"Shh, baby doll," he soothed, rubbing my back.

"I love you so damn much," I cried.

"I love you, too."

"I know," I hiccupped, squeezing him tight. "That's why I'm crying. 'Cause you're just so... perfect."

"I'm not perfect," he laughed, pulling back so he could see my face. "Far from it."

I lifted my hand and ran my palm down one of his cheeks to cup his jaw. "But you're perfect for me."

"You can't say shit like that right now," he groaned with a quick glance at the clock on my nightstand. "We only have a couple hours until they get home."

"Sounds like just enough time to say goodbye to my bed to me, don't you think?"

"One last time," he rasped, tearing at my clothes. My hands trembled as I did the same with his, desperate for both of us to be naked as quickly as possible so we could make the most of the limited time we had.

Once all our clothes were scattered across the floor, Harrison tossed me onto the mattress, yanking me down until my ass was at the edge before he sank to his knees in front of me. Then he bent my legs, placing my feet on the mattress and spreading me open for his touch. He didn't waste any time once he got me into the position he wanted; he just lowered his head and went straight for my clit, sucking it into his mouth.

"Yes, yes, yes," I chanted as he nibbled on my clit and thrust a finger inside me.

He knew my body so well, having spent the last two weeks learning every inch of it. In the matter of a couple of minutes, my stomach started to tighten as I writhed in his grip. With his hands tightening on my ass, he growled against me and the vibrations sent me over the edge.

"Mine," he growled against my wet flesh after licking me through my orgasm.

Rising to his feet, standing at the edge of the bed, he lifted my hips higher and wrapped my legs around his hips. His cock nudged at my entrance, but he didn't move to take me like he normally would. Instead, he held his lower body still as he bent lower, until his mouth was over mine. His tongue slid inside and caressed mine slowly. I could taste myself on him, mixed with the flavor that was uniquely Harrison. His kiss was a leisurely exploration, slow and soft, that had my heart racing for a completely different reason than the usual when we were naked and in bed with each other.

It was... more. More heartfelt. More meaningful. Just more.

"Love you," I whispered.

"I love you, too, baby doll. More than anything in the world," he murmured as he slowly slid inside me.

With our eyes locked, he circled his hips before he withdrew from my body.

"You make me so damn happy." He plunged back in.

"Me too," I gasped as he pulled out and rammed back in.

"Can't wait to live in that little blue cottage with you. To spend each night together just like this, until you graduate from school and we can go on an adventure together." His voice was raspy as he murmured against my lips, grinding his pelvis against me as his cock surged deep inside.

"My first," I panted, my body already tightening in pleasure again.

"Another first. I want them all."

"You've got them, Harrison. Anything you want from me, it's yours."

"Your sweet cherry, your ass, your mouth wrapped around my cock," he rattled off, hips pumping and eyes burning with desire.

"You've already had two of the three."

"Your first smile of each day, your first road trip, first airplane flight, first trip out of the country," he continued.

"All yours." I circled my hips, trying to get him to hit just the right spot since I was so close to coming.

"The first and only time you say 'I do.' Our first baby. Everything."

"Like I said, whatever you want from me is yours. But please, if you love me, let me come!" I had reached the point of mindless desperation.

"When I propose for real, I'm going to remind you that you already said yes," he warned me as his lips twisted into a satisfied smirk. Then he gave me exactly what I needed, pumping in and out of me as his hand slid in between us until his finger was able to circle my clit. I flew apart screaming his name. My nails digging into his back as I drew his body as close to me as I could get him.

"Yes," he hissed out on his next thrust, my pussy clenching around his cock. His body went rigid, and he tumbled into oblivion with me.

I felt closer to him than I ever had before. All was right in the world, cocooned away from everything else with his arms wrapped around me and his cock deep inside me. It was the most beautiful moment we'd had together... right up until I heard my mom's startled cry.

My head jerked towards the noise, and I found her and Stanley standing in the doorway. Harrison and I had been so wrapped up in each other, we hadn't heard them return.

"Oh crap!" I yelped.

Harrison moved quickly, yanking the bedspread over us and rolling to make sure I was completely covered. "Out!" he roared, when he looked over his shoulder and saw that they were both still standing there, staring at us with shocked looks on their faces.

"Oh dear," my mom breathed out, jumping back to slam the door shut.

I didn't hear another word from my mom, which was completely out of the ordinary for her. She always had something to say, which meant we'd managed to shock her speechless.

Stanley, on the other hand, knocked roughly on the door.

"Magnolia, I think it would be best if Harrison came down and talked to me alone. I'll send your mom up to you so she can make sure you're okay." His voice was stern but not harsh, until he spoke to Harrison and it became jagged and fury filled. "Harrison, get your ass out of my daughter's bed and downstairs. Now."

"Oh shit," I moaned once I heard his footsteps moving away and tears filled my eyes.

"Hush, baby doll. Everything's going to be fine."

"Fine? Fine!" I squealed. "How is anything ever going to be fine again? My mom and step-dad just saw us having sex!"

"No, they saw us after we'd just finished," he corrected.

I pushed on his chest and scurried off the mattress to grab my clothes from the floor. Throwing them on, I kept muttering to myself. "That's basically the same thing. You were naked. I was naked. Your dick was inside me. This is not how I wanted to break the news to them."

"Maggie," he snapped, snagging my attention. "Our relationship is good news, not something you have to break to them. Does it suck that they found out this way? Yes. Is it the end of the world? No. Nothing's really changed. I love you. You love me. At the end of today, we're going to climb into our bed together, just like we always will from now on."

"But my mom—"

"Your mom loves you and wants you to be happy. She'll come around once she realizes that we belong together."

Logically, I knew he was right. Plus, my mom had always been unconventional, so her daughter falling in love with her new brother-in-law was something she might come to accept sooner than most parents would. Hopefully. But her new husband? Not so much. "And Stanley?"

"He might be harder to convince"— Harrison pulled his shirt over his head and stalked towards me—"considering the size of the stick up his ass. But I've seen the way he looks at your mom. Hopefully, falling in love with her will have softened him up a little bit."

"That hardly sounds optimistic."

He stole my lips for a quick, but deep, kiss. "I love my brother, but I'm not going to let him, or anyone else, stand between me and you."

"Agreed." I gripped his hand firmly in mine and reached for the door with my other hand. "We do this together."

I just wished it didn't feel like we were off to face a firing squad.

Chapter 11
Harrison

I opened the door to Maggie's bedroom to find Bunny pacing and wringing her hands. She stopped suddenly and stared at us, wide-eyed. When her eyes met mine, she shook her head, disappointment washing over her face.

She moved towards Maggie, but I pulled her into my side, refusing to leave her behind. "We'll discuss this all together, Bunny," I informed her, my tone making it clear I was going to be unbending on this issue. "I'm not going to leave Maggie to face either of you alone."

Bunny's expression softened just the tiniest bit, but she locked eyes with Maggie and asked, "Are you okay?"

"I'm great, Mom," Maggie assured her. "This was my choice. No one forced me or coerced me."

Bunny hesitated for a few moments more, her eyes bouncing between us warily. Then she turned and silently descended the stairs.

Maggie looked up at me, her blue eyes swimming with unshed tears. I kissed her lovingly and whispered, "Trust me, baby doll." Her lips tipped up and some of the fear receded.

Keeping her hand in mine, I led her down the stairs to the living room. Bunny had taken a seat on the couch, but Stanley was pacing in front of the television across the room. He halted when we entered the room and when he noticed Maggie, he glared at me.

"Bunny, would you please take Magnolia to another room so Harrison and I can talk?" he asked her calmly. His tone and general demeanor were calm anyway, his eyes were spitting fire at me. "She shouldn't have to witness this, nor should Harrison be able to hide behind a child," he spit.

"No," Maggie piped up. "I'm staying. And, I'd like to point out, *once again*, that I am eighteen. An *adult,* not a child. I was an adult long before I turned eighteen and it's time everyone started treating me like it."

Stanley's expression became a little rueful. "You're right, Magnolia. But, you're still too young for my much older brother to be taking advantage of you." His brown eyes shifted to me and all the softness fled from his face. "I've never been so disappointed in you, Harrison. I always thought I raised you better than this. I trusted you with my daughter and come home to find you've taken advantage of an innocent girl!"

I'd had enough. "Stanley, I'm going to need you to shut it and listen to what we have to say."

His lips pressed together in a straight line and his face flushed with anger, but he didn't continue. I nodded and led Maggie over to the love seat. We both sat and I tucked her into my side, ignoring the daggers poking from Stanley's eyes.

"I didn't come here with the intention of seducing Maggie and that's not what happened. I fell for her the moment we met"—I held up my hand for silence when Stanley opened his mouth. He harrumphed, but didn't speak—"and before you accuse me, we waited until after she turned eighteen."

"It was the same for me, Stanley," Maggie interjected. "I knew the day he showed up that I loved him."

"Love?" Bunny gasped. Her eye brightened and she smiled at Maggie, almost dreamily.

"Yes, I love him, Mom," she confirmed.

"And I am completely head over heels in love with your daughter, Bunny."

She clasped her hands in front of her and sighed.

Stanley sputtered, "What about college? And—and, you can't possibly continue your ridiculous lifestyle, constantly leaving Magnolia and—You're not what she needs, Harrison."

"Honey, don't you think that's for Magnolia to decide?" Bunny asked quietly. "Look at them, Stanley. Really look. It's obvious they're in love."

"But, his lifestyle and..." Stanley was obviously incredulous that Bunny wasn't backing him up.

"Besides," she continued. "Magnolia's right. I'm ashamed to admit it, but she's been taking care of me her whole life. It's her turn to have freedom. Even if what she and Harrison have doesn't last"—I growled, but calmed when Maggie's hand landed on my thigh—"she deserves the opportunity to make her own mistakes."

Irritation was blooming in my chest at her referring to my relationship with Maggie as a mistake.

"I don't think that's what this is though, honey." Bunny stood and walked to Stanley, wrapping her arms around him.

"He looks at my girl the way you look at me."

Stanley seemed speechless, staring at Bunny as though he would find the answers to all the mysteries of the world in her eyes. After a minute, he looked rather resigned, but when his head lifted and he looked at me, there was still a hard quality on his face.

"I won't allow you to break her heart, Harrison. And, making her fall in love with you, only to leave her behind, is something only a jackass would do."

I nodded. "You're absolutely right." Stanley was taken aback by my answer, clearly he hadn't been expecting it. "That's why I'm staying here until Maggie graduates. I have some assignments lined up that are all close enough to complete on a weekend, when I can take my woman with me."

"Stanley," Bunny said quietly. "You've always been so proud of Harrison. Ever since I met you, you've shown how much you loved him. Do you really think he isn't good enough for our girl? That he wouldn't take care of her or that he'd mistreat her?"

He thought for a moment, then turned his contemplative stare to me. "No," he admitted, almost reluctantly, making me bite off a smile. He hated to be wrong, but that didn't mean he wouldn't own up to it when it happened. "I know the man I raised. Besides, our sweet Magnolia can't help but make him a better man."

Maggie jumped up and hurried over to hug her mom and Stanley. "He still isn't good enough for you," he said gruffly.

She laughed. "Will anybody ever be?"

"No." Stanley smiled and kissed her forehead, making me frown and stand up. I quickly grasped Maggie's arm and tugged her back against me.

"Keep your lips to yourself, brother," I warned darkly.

Bunny and Maggie laughed, but Stanley was less amused. His lips did tip up, though, and he tightened his embrace around Bunny.

"What about school?" he asked.

"I'm going to travel with Harrison for a while, Stanley," Maggie responded.

He looked like he wanted to argue, but Bunny came to the rescue once again. "She's young, honey. She has plenty of time to decide what she wants to do. It'll be good for her to get out of this little town and see the world."

"What about—"

"Honey." Bunny rolled her eyes and stood on her tip toes to kiss his chin. "Let it go."

Stanley sighed and nodded. "Don't expect me to stop worrying about her or checking in to make sure you're treating her right," he barked at me. "If you hurt her, you'll be singing soprano for the rest of your life."

I didn't laugh. It was an epic struggle, but I didn't laugh. I stuck my hand out. "Deal." We shook and Maggie sighed happily, reaching out a hand to her mom. We all stood there for a few awkward minutes, and seeing as how that was already the atmosphere, I figured it was as good a time as any to bring up another awkward subject. Not for me, but it was sure to make my sweet Maggie blush.

I cleared my throat. "Since Maggie is eighteen and I refuse to sleep without her, we figured it would be best to find our own place."

"Oh, but—" Bunny started to protest.

"Bunny." I gave her a knowing smile. "You and Maggie are similar in a lot of ways, and from the stupid look on Stanley's face after you've been alone together, as well as the frequency of those instances, I can only imagine that she inherited her passionate nature from you."

Maggie's fingers dug into my ribs, but I ignored the warning.

"I don't think anyone wants a repeat of what happened earlier."

Stanley's faced turned red with embarrassment, pretty much matching the color of Maggie's when I glanced down at her. Bunny however, threw her head back and laughed hysterically.

Stanley frowned. "Until she has a ring on her finger, you will sleep in the guest room and she will sleep in her bedroom while you are in this house," he commanded.

"I figured you'd say that and I respect your wishes," I countered. He looked mollified by my acceptance. "That's why we've already found a place and started moving into it."

Again, Stanley sputtered, but eventually, his face registered acceptance. He looked at Maggie. "I love you as though you were my blood daughter, Magnolia. Your mom and I will always be here for you."

Maggie and Bunny both beamed at him while I breathed a sigh of relief that everything had worked out. I was sick of hiding things and I was ready to get my woman to our house and christen every room, making sure the walls were all embedded with the sound of her screams.

"Thanks, Stanley. That means a—" Maggie halted mid-sentence and her hand flew to cover her mouth. Then she took off running. I followed right behind, entering the bathroom just as she dropped to the floor in front of the toilet and lost her breakfast.

Well fuck. That was fast. I hid my grin as I knelt beside her and held back her hair. Bunny handed me a damp wash cloth while she and Stanley stood worriedly in the doorway.

Maggie sat back after it seemed there was nothing left and I wiped down her face with the cool rag. I looked up at the couple in the doorway. "Could we have a minute?"

Bunny dragged Stanley away and shut the door. I grabbed a cup of water and handed it to Maggie, which she took gratefully. "I wonder if the sushi from last night was bad," she mused.

"I'm not sick," I reminded her, since we'd both eaten it.

"Oh, right." She seemed lost in thought for a minute and I wondered if I would have to spell it out for her. Then her eyes widened and her mouth formed a little O. "I couldn't be..." she denied, shaking her head.

"Baby doll," I sighed. "I've been fucking you without a condom for two weeks. A lot. I'm surprised it happened this fast, but with the amount of come I've filled you with, I probably shouldn't be." Her cheeks pinkened and I couldn't help chuckling.

"But what about our plans?" She seemed torn between being happy and worried.

"We'll make it work, sweet Maggie. I'm going to give you everything you ever wanted. If that means taking a nanny with us all around the world, that's what we'll do."

A bright smile creased her face and she never looked more beautiful to me. "I love you," she grinned happily.

"Damn good thing since I'm never letting you go."

"Fuck! You're so tight!" I panted as I bucked my hips, my cock dragging along the walls of her pussy. "Nobody but me can hear you, baby doll. Let me hear how much you want me to make you come."

"Yes! Please, Harrison! Oh, yes!"

She was so fucking hot when she begged. I sucked one turgid nipple into my mouth and gave it a deep pull. Her back arched and she cried out. "I want to live inside this pussy, baby doll," I growled, fucking her harder. My balls were drawing up and my spine was tingling. I wouldn't be able to hold out much longer.

I felt wilder tonight, almost feral. It seemed to be fueled by the knowledge that I'd done my job as a man and knocked up my woman. It was a good thing that we waited to take the test until we'd gotten to our place because the second it came up positive, I was on her.

I slid my hands up her arms and wrapped her fingers around the headboard. "Hold on tight." She gripped it and I moved my hands to her ass, lifting her and tightening her legs around my waist. Then I planted my fists into the bed, elbows locked, and dug my feet into the mattress for leverage. I began pounding into her so hard the bed slammed into the wall over and over.

"Yes! Yes! Yes!" she screamed.

"Oh fuck! Squeeze that pussy, Maggie. Yes! Fuck!"

Dropping my head, I took her mouth in a rough, tongue twisting kiss and it pushed her over the edge with me following right behind.

It took a while for us to come back down and when we did, I was still hard as a fucking rock. I flipped us over, still buried inside her so she was straddling me. "Ride me, baby doll," I commanded gruffly. I held her hips and guided her into a steady rhythm of rising and falling on my cock. Her gorgeous fat tits were bouncing in my face and I was mesmerized by the sight.

My hands slid around to cup her plump ass cheeks and I jerked her into me so I was hitting all the right spots every time she fell back down on my shaft. My eyes dropped to her flat belly and just like that, I exploded inside her with a roar. My orgasm fed hers and she screamed my name as she splintered apart.

Later, we cuddled in bed, her naked body sprawled across mine and my hands rubbing lazy circles on her back. I was still deep inside her, despite being only semi-hard. I couldn't bring myself to separate from her.

"When are we going to tell them about the baby?" Maggie inquired softly. "Aren't you supposed to wait until the third month or something?"

She was probably right, but I knew myself better than that. I wouldn't be able to hold out that long. "How about we tell them next weekend? We'll have them over for dinner to celebrate and tell them then."

She placed her hands on my chest and lifted up to look at my face. "What will they think we're celebrating?"

I reached to my left and opened the nightstand drawer, pulling out a little velvet pouch. "I was thinking that we could celebrate our engagement," I told her as I dangled it in front of her by the drawstrings.

Maggie gasped and stared at the little bag as it spun around. But, she made no move to take it.

"Well?" I said impatiently.

She raised an eyebrow and looked down her nose haughtily. "What?" she snapped without real malice. "Don't you have something to ask me before I open my present?"

I laughed, making Maggie's body bounce on me and her walls clamped down on my cock in a reflexive action, making me instantly hard. I groaned and rocked against her.

Maggie snapped her fingers in my face. "Focus, Harrison!"

I couldn't help chuckling again. "You are so fucking cute. You know that?" Her face glowed with pleasure, but she shrugged nonchalantly.

Opening the pouch, I dumped a sparkling diamond ring into my waiting palm. "Magnolia Rose Bloom, I love you more than anything. I want the world to know without any doubt that you are mine, will always be mine. Will you marry me?"

"Yes!" Maggie squealed and dove down for a deep, wet kiss. By the time she pulled back, we were both moaning from the friction where we were still joined. I slipped the ring on her finger and proceeded to make her give me the same one word answer over and over again throughout the night.

Epilogue
Maggie

The clicking of his camera alerted me to Harrison's presence before anything else did. It was a sound I'd quickly grown familiar with since he always seemed to have it in hand whenever we went on a trip. Cracking my eyes open, I placed a hand on my forehead to block out the sun so I could see his face when I looked up. "You're back!"

"I sure am," he confirmed, flashing me a devastating grin as his gaze swept up and down my swimsuit-clad body. "And you're a sight for sore eyes."

His eyes darted to the pool, scanning it quickly, before his smile turned into a frown. "Where are the girls?"

"Off learning about traditional dances with Amara." I pointed up at the balcony overlooking the pool. Two little blonde heads were barely visible, but Amara's eyes were latched onto them as they all moved to the music that drifted down towards the pool. She was one of the babysitters on staff at the lodge, and she'd been a life saver for me over the past month. "They wore me out and leapt at the chance to dance their little hearts out for a little bit while Mommy took a quick nap."

Harrison crouched low, resting a hand on my still-flat lower belly. "It's a good thing we're heading home soon. I'll feel better about the pregnancy once we can get you in to see your doctor."

"There's nothing to worry about," I reassured him. "I'm not that far along. There isn't anything for the doctor to even do yet, except to tell me I'm pregnant, and we've already confirmed it with that test you got me. Although, I'm still not sure how you managed to get your hands on one while we're in the middle of the Serengeti."

We were hours away from anything, surrounded by vast Acacia-studded grassland savannahs, riverine forests, swamps, hills and valleys. The lodge where we'd been staying was gorgeous, but the main attraction for most visitors were the countless species of wild animals and birds in the area. When Harrison had been invited to serve as the photojournalism expert for a well-respected African photo safari company, I'd begged him to say yes.

It was a great opportunity since he only had to accompany one group for nine days and provide them with a behind-the-scenes perspective during their trip.

We'd arrived in Africa two weeks early, giving us plenty of time to explore with Ginger and Rose. Ages two and four, they were quite the seasoned world travelers since we made it our mission to take them on trips several times a year. It started with an extended tour of Italy on an extended honeymoon, although, I hadn't gotten the champagne Harrison had promised me since I was four months pregnant with Rose at the time. Since then, we'd been to ten different countries on four continents—well, five now since we'd finally made it to Africa.

"Are you really surprised?" he asked. "You needed the test, so I made sure you had it."

"Like always." It had been like that since the day we met, Harrison doing whatever it took to take care of me. Making my dreams come true with all the adventures a girl could want and the growing family I'd always dreamed about. "But this time around, you get to tell my mom and step-dad that you knocked me up again."

"Bunny will be thrilled," he chuckled, knowing damn well that he was right. My mom had taken to the role of grandma like she was born to it. "But I have a feeling Stanley is going to threaten my balls."

"That's what you get for getting me pregnant while we're in the wilds of Africa. You know how worried he gets, especially when we take the girls with us." Stanley was an amazing grandfather to the our daughters, but he was also quite the worrywart—which he liked to say was because he had to do double duty as their uncle too. "And if it's finally a boy this time, I just might let him have your balls since we won't need them anymore."

"Oh, yeah?" he huffed.

I cocked my head at him sassily before giggling. "Maybe not. I think I might want one more out of you either way."

"Whatever you want, baby doll."

Little did we know, he'd already given me the boy I wanted, along with another baby girl. Fraternal twins to round out our family.

Books By This Author

RISQUÉ CONTRACTS SERIES

Penalty Clause

Contingency Plan

Fraternization Rule

YEAH, BABY SERIES

Baby, You're Mine

Baby Steps

Baby, Don't Go

Dance With Me, Baby

I'm Yours, Baby

Brief Me, Baby

MAFIA TIES: NIC & ANNA

Deception

Danger

Devotion

MAFIA TIES: BRANDON & CARLY

Pursuit

Power

Passion

About the Author

The writing duo of Elle Christensen and Rochelle Paige team up under the Fiona Davenport pen name to bring you sexy, insta-love stories filled with alpha males. If you want a quick & dirty read with a guaranteed happily ever after, then give Fiona Davenport a try!

You can also connect with Fiona online on Facebook or Twitter.

Made in the USA
Coppell, TX
20 March 2022

75292074R00073